CH

After the Death
of Anna Gonzales

TERRI FIELDS

After the Death
of Anna Gonzales

Henry Holt and Company
New York

Henry Holt and Company, LLC
Publishers since 1866
115 West 18th Street
New York, New York 10011
www.henryholt.com

Library of Congress Cataloging-in-Publication Data
Fields, Terri.
After the death of Anna Gonzales / Terri Fields.
p.   cm.
Summary: Poems written in the voices of forty-seven people, including students,
teachers, and other school staff, record the aftermath of a high school student's
suicide and the preoccupations of teen life.
1. Young adult poetry, American. 2. Teenagers—Suicidal behavior—Poetry.
3. High school students—Poetry. 4. Suicide victims—Poetry. 5. Teenagers—
Poetry. [1. Suicide—Poetry. 2. High schools—Poetry. 3. Schools—Poetry.
4. American poetry.] I. Title.
PS3556.I42115 A689 2002   811'.54—dc21   2002024074

ISBN 0-8050-7127-X
First Edition—2002
Printed in the United States of America on acid-free paper. ∞

10 9 8 7 6 5 4 3 2 1

Permission for the use of the following is gratefully acknowledged:

Excerpt from "The End of the World," from *Collected Poems*, 1917–1982,
by Archibald MacLeish. Copyright © 1985 by the Estate of Archibald MacLeish.
Reprinted by permission of Houghton Mifflin Company.
All rights reserved.

Excerpt from "Do Not Go Gentle into That Good Night" by Dylan Thomas, from
The Poems of Dylan Thomas, published by New Directions. Copyright © 1952 by
Dylan Thomas. Reprinted by permission of New Directions Publishing Corp.

To Life

*With love for those
who make my life special:
Mom, Rick, Lori, Larry, and Jeff*

*And with gratitude for
excellent manuscript advice from
Erin Murphy, Christy Ottaviano,
and Rick and Jeff Fields*

After the Death
of Anna Gonzales

Lisa McNair

I can feel
The whispering of the hallway walls
Growing louder as the groups gather.
Each clique adding its morning input.

> *"Did you hear?"*
> *"Who told you?"*
> *"Do you think it's really true?"*

New at this school,
I stand alone.

Watching . . .
A group of girls plot
For Homecoming only days away.

> *"He might ask . . ."*
> *"Try to run into him."*
> *"No one is wearing purple."*
> *"But if Julio goes with Gina, then . . ."*

Seeing . . .
A brown-eyed boy aim a slight nod and slow smile
At a green-eyed girl.
Who seems not to see him but somehow moves closer.

"Hey."
  "Hey yourself."

Hearing . . .
A boy beg for finished algebra homework to copy.
Hoping someone will save him.

  "No time to do it."
    "Impossible anyway."
  "Teacher's a witch."

My first week at this school.
Seeing but not really being seen.
Trying to figure out how I will fit in.

Listening to the rhythms of this new place.
Already I am able to pick up some familiar refrains.

Yet sandwiched among this morning's murmurs
Today's hallway hints at something more horrible.

  "I heard . . ."
    "Who was it?"
  "How'd she do it?"
    "Wonder if it hurt?"
  "Anyone know why?"

The gossip gets grabbed by Senior Square.

> *"Found out it was just some freshman."*
> *"Did she leave a note?"*
> *"Don't know."*
> *"Probably not true."*
> *"Stupid."*

> *"I think about it once in . . ."*

The blaring of the bell.

> Lockers slam.
> Students scatter.

And I start another day at this new school . . . wondering.

Principal Barron

Thirty years in education.
I've broken up fights.
Fired a teacher.
Failed a student.
But not this.
This is too much to ask.

> "Volleyball practice has been moved to 5:00 P.M.
> The chess club will meet today in
> Mr. Malkin's room."

Thirty years in education.
I've learned school law.
Listened to angry parents.
Located lost school buses.
But not this.
This is too much to ask.

> "Congratulations to the JV football team on last
> night's 14–0 win against the Raiders.
> Student Council will be selling spirit T-shirts
> during both lunch hours all week."

To make a difference.
To better kids' lives.
That was why I went into education.

So how does this happen?
How do I . . .

"Mr. Barron, announcements are almost over.
Do you still have a special?"

I trudge toward the camera.

"And now for a special from our principal."

Words caught in unwilling voice.

"I am sorry to tell you of the death
of one of our students."

Must continue.
Rumors always worse than truth.

"Anna Gonzales took her life last night.
Our sympathies to her family and friends.
Grief counselors will be available all day."

Robotlike move off camera.
As a chirpy voice concludes,

"And those are today's announcements.
Have a nice day."

Damon Reingold

The game doesn't always go your way.
I know.
You can go to every practice
Even when your shoulder aches
      Your ankle throbs
      Your homework waits.
You can do 100 hand-offs
      1,000 free throws
      10,000 reps
And still sit on the bench
    While
You watch Darrith Evans
      Slack off
      Skip practice
      Showboat for Debbie
And still be part of the
      Starting five.

The game doesn't always go your way.
      Forget fair.
      Feel forgotten.
But damn it, Anna,

      You don't stop playing.

Manuel Ramirez

I'm on my way to class.
Tardy bell hasn't even rung.
When Mrs. Bernstein, the scholarship aide,
Stops me and calls me into her office.

"Manuel," she says, "do you think of yourself as mature?"
        "I guess . . ."
"Do you think of yourself as intelligent?"
        I shrug—"My grades are pretty good."
"Do you think you're a good representative of this school?"
        I have no idea what she's getting at.

"Well, we do," she continues.
School announcements start.
Mrs. Bernstein turns them off.
"What I'm trying to tell you is
That's why the faculty submitted your name
For the National Future Leader Award."

        "The what?" I ask.

"Remember I asked you for your government essay?
We submitted it and five faculty recommendations.
I didn't say anything to you because
We've never had a winner here before . . .

"But, Manuel, you won!" she says.
"You're going to Washington, D.C., for a whole week,
    all expenses paid."

    "Wow!" I manage to croak.
    I've never even been out of this city before.

"Congratulations!" She smiles and hands me a stack
    of papers.

In a daze, I walk into my first-hour class,
Put the pass on Mrs. Johnson's desk,
And feel my face flaunting an ever-growing grin
As I begin what has already been
The best day of my life.

Kathleen Hays

My brother was seven
When they told us the bad news:
It was a tumor
That had bloomed in his body
Like a weed.

Seven surgeries, and still he smiled.
We had his eighth birthday party in the hospital.
He said he could feel that he was almost well.
And we celebrated.

At nine, they said new cells had sprouted.
The chemo was strong.
The cancer was stronger.

But . . . in spite of the pills and the pain,
In spite of the surgeries and suffering,
He chose life.

And you, Anna, who had health,
Chose death.

How could you?

Jason Foley

"Life's rough, and then you die."

That's what the sign above the restaurant sink
Says in big red letters.
Only there's a grease spot that covers the *i*.

I work kitchen clean-up
Illegally because I'm too young,
But they pay me in cash
And I hide most of it from my dad
So he won't drink it away.

It took me seventeen days and three hours
To earn enough
For my fine new shoes.
But they were definitely worth it.

I don't know who stole 'em—yet.
But I will.
Believe it.

And when I do,
I'll take care of things.
Know it.

Meanwhile, I work and watch the big red letters
That say
"Life's rough, and then you die,"
And I think,
Not me.
        Not yet.

Francine Bradishio

I will not talk when the teacher is talking.
I will not talk when the teacher is talking.
I will not talk when the teacher is talking.
I will not talk when the teacher is talking.
I will not talk when the teacher is talking.
I will not talk when the teacher is talking.
I will not talk when the teacher is talking.
I will not talk when the teacher is talking.
I will not talk when the teacher is talking.
I will not talk when the teacher is talking.
I will not talk when the teacher is talking.
I will not talk when the teacher is talking.
I will not talk when the teacher is talking.
I will not talk when the teacher is talking.
I will not talk when the teacher is talking.
I will not talk when the teacher is talking.

My wrist hurts.
My thumb is numb.
And the pain in my fingers is fierce.

God . . . I still have 434 sentences to do before
fourth hour.

When Mrs. Ebert assigned them yesterday,
She said, "I hope this teaches you a lesson."

And it has.

There's no way I'm getting in trouble for talking in
English again.
As soon as I get to class today, I'm going straight
to sleep.

Ricky Stevens

Me.
The one
Who always does just what adults expect.

Referred to as
      Responsible.
        Obedient.
          Boring.

     Until today.

When I took the checkered flag.
And left behind Mom and Dad's
Lists of "notes for when we're out of town."
Which, by the way, never actually said,
"You cannot take Dad's new Corvette!"

Now, as I sit through these never-ending
    announcements,
I can still feel my hands gripping the wheel.
My foot flooring the gas.

I'll be free again at three,
To ease back into the soft black leather seats

And downshift into the winds of
Unpredictable.
Incompliant.
Exciting.

Wonder if I should offer Lynn a ride?

Lauren Reynolds

Since September,
I sat one seat behind Anna in algebra.
Passed papers to her every day.
Studied for tons of tests together.

Though it often seemed impossible,
Eventually,
We always found the unknown for X.

But not this time.
This equation
Bounces against my brain.
And sneers at all attempted answers.

I know I'll re-examine the variables,
And reanalyze the unknowns, maybe forever.
But
It won't matter.

Because, Anna—
I know I'll never figure out Y.

Y you didn't want to live—
And Y I never noticed.

Debbie Hill

We agreed.
Together, all ten.
We'd stand in a line,
And on the downbeat we all kick at exactly the
    same height.
But not Emily.

She always makes sure her leg lifts a little higher
    than mine.
Does she think I don't notice?
She says she just doesn't know why
Her sweater fits so perfectly,
And wonders why mine looks a little baggy.
The answer is easy.
She shrank hers until it became a second skin.

She thinks she's flashy.
I think she's trashy.

She does her high kicks for Darrith.
Let her.
I don't dance for him or anyone else.

Music just makes me want to move.
The downbeat begins,

And the adrenaline rushes.
The crowd becomes a blur.

Oops, the announcements ended.
So how come everyone's just sitting here so quietly?
It's only English.
Boring, but
It's not like somebody died or anything.

Darrith Evans

I can picture it all now:

Me: Coach, I'm sorry, but I just don't feel right
           about practicing today.

Coach: *But we've got a big game tomorrow.*

Me: Coach, I won't let you down.
           I'll be there.
           You can count on me.
           But today . . .
           I just can't—
           I mean, Anna . . .

Coach: *I didn't know you knew her.*

Me: (looking down at the floor—catch in my voice)
           I do have a life outside of basketball.

Coach: *(putting his hand on my shoulder)*
           I'm sorry, son.
           Skip the practice.
           Go be with the Gonzales family.

Anna Gonzales, I never knew you.

Although you were probably in the stands
Watching me play.

I'm sorry you took your life.
But I can't get it back for you.
So you might as well help me.

See, I just cannot make Coach understand
That unlike most
Of the guys on our team
I don't need all these practice sessions.
I always come through in the games.
So why can't Coach just let me be?

Andrea Brensk

In seventh-hour Spanish,
Anna Gonzales sat in the second row, second seat.
How do I know?
Every day, I wished I could trade places with her.

Spanish is the only class I have with Chad Alexander.
That most gorgeous and very shy guy.
I don't think Anna ever noticed him.
Even though in group work
        She always got paired with Chad.

Me—
I'm stuck on the other side of the room.
        With god-awful Greg Mendez.
        And his ox-snorting laugh.

So I'm wondering if today is too soon
To ask Ms. Alvarez if I could switch seats.
I mean . . .
I don't want anyone to think I'm insensitive.

But I don't want to miss the moment.
And have someone else sneak into the seat that should
    be mine.

I know that I could find the right language
For me and Chad.
If I could just improve our geography.

Chad Alexander

Anna Gonzales . . .

There's an Anna in my Spanish class.
A million times we said *"¿Cómo te llamas?"*
But we never answered with last names.
Still, somehow I think it might be her.

Suicide . . .

Anna seemed normal enough,
But how much can you know
When working together to conjugate
The present tense of *hablar*?

If it is the same Anna, her seat's gonna be empty.
Not just absent empty—but forever empty.
Weird.
        Very weird.
                Too weird.

Maybe Mark could move into that seat.
Then we could do Spanish skits about baseball.
"Uno, dos, tres strikes and you *vamos* from the old
    ball game."
It would make seventh hour *más bueno*.

Otherwise, this girl Andrea may try to move there.
Fourteen of her friends have told me she likes me
A lot.
She sits in the back of the room, but she's always
Giggling and staring at me.
I pretend not to notice.

She'd be better off with Greg.
Geeks like those two
Really should stick together.

Actually, I hope . . .

Anna will be in her seat seventh hour
And life will go on, just like it's supposed to.

I guess Anna didn't find out that you could opt out
Without really leaving.
I did
       A long time ago.

The rest of my family is the roaring center of success.
And the model for superstress.

My dad is the proud owner of four fine classic cars,
Which no one ever drives.
In number, they match his four heart attacks.

My mom is #1 in sales
Again.
And my older sister's straight A's are delivered
As expected.

My family feels that
The entrance to our house is
The driveway to the top.

BELIEVE!
ACHIEVE!

And I—
Realizing I could never compete on any other level—
Have become their number one failure.

Actually, I'm very good at doing nothing.
And so, declaring my own sort of victory,
I long ago opted out of their high-stakes game.

Andy Gotchalder

Get out our homework?
You gotta be kidding, Mrs. Johnson!
How can we just go over algebra
Like nothin' happened or anything.
Shouldn't we be like . . . I don't know,
Shouldn't we be quiet or something this hour?

Yeah, well, I am a sensitive guy,
I just get a bad rap.
Maybe we could put on music and think . . .
You know . . .
I've got a good CD.

What?
       Turn in our homework and then we can
       Have time to reflect?
My homework?
       Well, I don't have it.
Where is it?
       Actually, I didn't do it.
Why not?
       Ah, come on, Mrs. Johnson, you know, last night
          was Thursday.
       And that's way too close to the weekend for
          homework.

Mrs. Johnson,
Algebra Teacher

Too many papers.
Too many meetings.
Too many students.

But I do try to reach them all.
In the limited time I have.

Yes, they sit in rows.
Yes, they figure numbers.
Yes, they fill in No. 2 pencil tests.

But it is the sum of who they are
That matters to me.
Haven't I shown them that?
Not well enough, I guess,
For poor Anna Gonzales is dead.

The class seems stunned.
Staring now at me
As if I should know an answer for
All of this.

And the only answer I know is
That no child should give up on life.
Math deals in absolutes.
But life is the most absolute of all.

John Morgan

It wasn't me that said, "Come on over tonight."
It wasn't me that said, "My parents aren't home."
And it wasn't me that said, "Want a beer?"
I mean I wasn't complaining,
But it wasn't me suggesting the horizontal
    communication,
If you know what I mean.

Hey, I don't mind being Kimmy's boy toy.
I'd be first to say that last night was a sweet gig.
But what's up with Sharlee this morning
Calling me a disgusting pig?
On account of what Kimmy told her.
Today,
I think maybe me and Kimmy better have
A little better vertical communication.

Sharlee Williams

Anna Gonzales—not sure I knew her.
But maybe she was motivated by a "best friend"
  like Kimmy.

Kimmy, who knew my every secret and insecurity,
Kimmy, who plotted with me for weeks
About the blow-out party we'd have
The minute her parents left town.

We counted the hours
Until our popularity plan.

So was the party a success?
No way.
At least not for me.

Her parents were barely out the door, before
Kimmy told me to get lost because (giggle)
John was coming over.
And the party had been downsized to two.

Dismissed just that fast,
I stayed home.
Feeling stupid and depressed
That my feelings meant nothing
To Kimmy.

I cried a lot and thought even more.
Then I redefined the word "friendship."

And this morning,
When I got to school,
I worked on a little revenge.

Kimmy Nelson

"She took her own life."
Is that what Mr. Barron said?
I was only half listening.
But I'm pretty sure I heard
"She took her own life."
Those were the words.
Inserted right near the end
Of our usually boring morning announcements.

Suicide.

Awful.
Really awful.

I'm so glad I've got a friend like Sharlee
And maybe even a boyfriend in John.
It would be awful to feel as alone as
Anna.

Carrie Sells

I keep trying to wrap my arms
Around my world
So that I can get some control over it.
I've tried to make the circle large enough
For my second stepdad, who taught me how to play
    baseball,
And my mom's new husband, who really wants us to
    be a family.
For my dad's ex-girlfriend, who taught me to make
    ice-cream pie,
And my dad's third wife, who was kind of like a sister
When I stayed with them.

I suppose I'm lucky.
Everyone wants to be in my world.
Eighth-grade graduation was only for immediate
    family,
And I needed sixteen tickets.

But I'm always in the role of peacemaker.
"Can't you all play nicely?"
I want to shout.

Still, it seems that no matter how large I make my circle
No one's ever happy.

Sometimes, when everyone is shouting at everyone,
And everyone expects me to make it right,
I think about killing myself,
Leaving a letter
That says to each one of these
"Grown-ups" who say they care so much,
"You can keep one little part of me.
                Put it on a shelf.
                        Hang it on a wall.
That part will be yours forever,
And no one will have to fight anymore."

But then I decide I don't want to die.
I haven't really even had my
Chance
To live.

So I just keep trying to make my arms grow,
Hoping that someday
I can put them around my world enough
To get control of it.

Eric Sueffert

If I could,
I would.
But I can't sneak out of this class right now.
So I'll have to wait.
Fifty more minutes for freedom,
Before I'm down the back staircase
And outta here.

I've got to get to Anna's house
In time to beat the rest of the media
That's bound to come.

Tonight, on *News at 10*,
Maybe, they'll feature my interview.

Okay . . .
So Mrs. Gonzales doesn't really know me.
        But I do go to Anna's school.
Okay . . .
So it's gonna be pretty weird going to her house today.
        But investigative reporters do hard stuff all the time.

My mom would say it's too rude.
But my mom doesn't understand.
Why should I wait until after college
When this could be my big break?

Damn! I wish I'd taken Anna to a dance.
Then I'd have had some special background.
Definitely a missed opportunity now.

Tammy Billet

I want to

> Safari into Africa and see zebras right up close.
> Sing with an all-girl band that rocks right off the
>   charts.
> Send myself to Paris for a summer on the Seine.
> Stay up all night dancing with a handsome,
>   mysterious man
> > Who kisses me passionately and sweeps
> > me off into the best of the romance
> > novels I read on the Saturdays I
> > spend alone.

Every time my father fails to provide child support,
And my mother cries that she doesn't know what to
    do about all these mouths
To feed,
I go in my room and add another line to my list.

I don't understand why anyone would think
That life isn't going to get better.
How could you check out
Before the good stuff ever started?

Alexis Jimers

I always thought I was so
Lucky
That my friend never spilled secrets
Like my crush on Ricky
Which she didn't let slip
Even when Debbie promised great gossip in return.

A and A they called us,
But we called ourselves the A+s.
Because that's how it seemed when we were
Together.

We spent sleepovers swearing Ms. Mason had a crush on
    Mr. Barron.
We wondered about the "right" way to really kiss a boy.
We made collages of all our favorite movie stars.
Once, we even invented our own language.

But somewhere, buried in all those words,
Must have been a meaning I didn't understand.
And somehow, lost in all those kept secrets,
Was one I'd give anything for her to have spoken.

I could always accept not being the prettiest or
    the smartest
Because I had the best of friends.
A and A they called us.
But, Anna, somehow, I failed you.
And now I've lost the best part of
Me.

Martin Martinez

Last year, me and Vinnie and Jorge
Were on the corner by the 7-Eleven.
We're just standin' there.
We weren't doing nothin'.
Just hangin' around.
When this white car goes by.
It had this blue kinda stripe.
And I thought, one day when I get my car,
I want a stripe like that.

The car drove by again.
I pointed to it.
Jorge said, "No way. That is u—g—ly!"
He started to say something else,
But there was this pop.
Jorge fell.
And the car sped off.

I held Jorge in my arms
As his white shirt turned red.
Jorge looked so scared.
"You're gonna be okay," I kept screaming.

At Jorge's funeral
His uncle said Jorge wanted to be a lawyer someday.

His mother said he wanted to be a priest someday.
His little sister said he wanted to be real rich someday.

But most of all,
I wanted and
I think he wanted
Just to be alive.

Lynn Helter

Oh my God.
Not this week.
Why did Anna have to kill herself now?

I don't mean to be rude or anything,
But
She certainly didn't have any consideration.

Everyone knows how important this pep assembly
    is going to be.
Tonight, we face our toughest game.
I have personally pushed to make this assembly great.
Unlike some people,
I take my responsibility to this school seriously.

It may seem easy to get the cheerleaders to go third.
But they're mad that the football team's introductions
    take up too much time.

And the coach, he just keeps saying,
"After all, Lynn, we wouldn't be having this assembly
    if it weren't for the team."

I tried to cut the ROTC's flag raising,
But that didn't fly with the principal.

All this work to make perfect pep.
And the assembly is for everyone.
So there better not be calls to cancel it now.
Because that's not going to happen.

Life goes on.

Look up,

Smile,

And feel the purple pride!

Shannon Delany

How do I feel about Anna?

I don't know.
She's always been in my classes.

First Grade
      Sounding out S's through our missing front teeth.
Third Grade
      Practicing perfect cursive C's and B's.
Fifth Grade
      Being part of the Famous Fraction Finders.

Sixth, Seventh, Eighth, Ninth Grades.

Counting up the details of all the classes we shared,
We learned
      The capital of North Dakota.
      The square root of 144.
      The definition of 1,000 vocabulary words.

But I guess lost in all that information,
No one ever taught Anna how to live,
And for sure,
No one taught me how to feel
About finding out how she died.

Mandy Krantz

Oh my God. I'm late again.
Ms. Mason is going to kill me.
    My alarm didn't go off.
    The power went out.
    The car had a flat.
    My bike was broken.
        Get real . . . I would ride a bike to school?

Okay. So think. There's gotta be a good excuse.
    A car hit my dog.
        Used it yesterday.
    My cat ran away.
        Already said the cat died last week.

Well, school shouldn't start so early.
Don't these people have a clue how much there is to do
   at night?

I'm here now . . . Can't that just be enough?
So . . . I'm just opening this door.
No excuses needed.

What's with all this silence and the faces?
Did I forget about a test?

Tiffany Gibson

Before Andy's party,
I took a few sips
From a whiskey bottle
In my parents' bar.
It burned my throat.
It made my eyes tear.
I hated it.
But it gave me the courage
To be an impostor.
To walk into Andy's party
Without my knees knocking.

But once I was there,
Once I was right in the middle of the popular kids,
It wasn't enough.

I was afraid
They'd discover I was a geek in disguise.

So I made myself guzzle the first can of beer.
The second just sort of slid right down.
I'm not sure when Andy challenged me
To match him can for can,
Or why I agreed.

I don't even remember taking off my top.
But I've seen the crude cartoons the guys have drawn,
So I must have done it.

One night.
One time to be part of the cool kids.
And now I walk through these school halls,
And I look at no one.
And I die a little each day as I live through it.

Jenna Etkin

So I'm failing geometry.
Doesn't matter.
I'm passing my other classes.

So there's no money for new clothes.
Doesn't matter.
I've got Goodwill.

So they disconnected the phone at our house.
Doesn't matter.
I've got a beeper.

So we've got a few extra people sleeping on the floor.
Doesn't matter.
At least we've got a floor to sleep on.

Hey,
Life only gets you down if you let it.

Ms. Mason,
English Teacher

"Death be not proud . . ."
"Do not go gentle into that good night . . ."

Fragments of poems I've taught.
Can't finish them—can't think how they go.
Brain too numb to truly believe.

That empty seat in the third row.
Anna will be back.
She must be.
Quiet, sweet . . .
A face framed by long lush brown hair.
Almond eyes always seemed luminous.
Giving no hint that this unnatural sleep would be
      her fate.

I've tried to teach through literature
The wonder of life.

Yet the quiet rebuke of that empty chair
Speaks louder than the most vocal of student skeptics.

I cannot take my eyes from the spot.
"There in the sudden blackness, the black pall
Of nothing, nothing, nothing—nothing at all."

Aaron Sherman

Shimmering and elusive
Stanford stands
atop a surface that few will reach.
Scores swim hysterically in schools of
           APs and SATs.
We gasp for breath in
           revised résumés and
           agonized essays

knowing all the while that
the brutal tide of competition
           and
           the bait of spare time
will force most back to
be more bottom feeders.

I cannot do that.
I will not drown.

Study don't sleep.
Study don't socialize.
Study don't loosen up.

Being number one still might
not be enough,
but it's a start.

Ms. Mason's face frowns as she hears about Anna.
"Don't postpone today's test!" I pray.
Tomorrow's a calculus test.
Tonight's for memorizing math.

PRESSURE.

It peels everything else away.

Randal Mallander

Anna—
> If only you had some idea of how
> Many times I went by your house
> Once walking almost to your door.

> Then, courage canceled, I crept away too
> Unwilling to risk your rejection.

From the first time I saw your big brown eyes,
I thought, "There's a girl I want to know."
And I hoped that one day
>> someday,
The right words would come.
And you would
See me and smile.

Now that will never be.

Still, I cannot quite believe
That those big brown eyes
Are forever closed.

Somehow, I feel almost blinded myself.
And I am forever left to wonder
Whether telling you how truly special
You were
Might have made a difference.

Mike Bradler

Okay, I've got ten bucks from Eric says I won't do it.
Matt says that goes double for him.
And Gary's in for another ten.
That almost pays for Homecoming.
But hey . . . even without the money . . . why not?

It's a whole *Staying Alive,* disco, '70s look
That I found in our attic.
White suit, shiny shirt.
Slicked hair.
Like Travolta before the fat.

So this morning I told Stephanie.
Said I thought we could sucker in a few more guys
If she'd dress up too.
"Hey, isn't life all about fun?" I asked.
And that's when she said,
"Grow up, Michael.
I just realized that
I've got the right dress,
But the wrong date!"

Girls.
How can God give 'em such great bodies
And take away their sense of humor
All at the same time?

Karen Covington

Mixed-up Memories
    Of the daddy
        Who introduced me to Winnie-the-Pooh.
        Who sang every verse of kids' silly songs.
        Who whispered the lullabies that lured me
           to sleep.

Mixed-up Memories
    Of the dad
        Who cheered my summer softball
           Even if I never got a hit.
        Who promised I would always be
           His most perfect princess.

Mixed-up Memories
    Of the father
        Who guaranteed he'd be the proudest of all
           the parents
           At my college graduation.
        Who vowed he'd walk me down the aisle
           even if I married at forty.
        Who predicted no one would be a better
           grandpa.

Mixed-up Memories
>   Of a morning last summer
>   When I learned
>   My hero had taken his own life.

When that was the truth,
Everything I understood of love and safety
Was a lie.

So, Anna, did you know
That when you kill yourself
Those you say you love,
They die too?

Kendra Jones

You don't have to be Someone
To be someone special.
You don't have to live the dream
To believe in the future of dreams.
Sometimes, I seem to forget that.

Bogged down in the stresses and stupidities of my life
I feel
        Insignificant in Jarod's indifference
        Forgotten by Francine's clique
        Betrayed by Brittany's gossip
        Imposed upon by my mother's edicts
        Battered by my teachers' busywork.

But I'm going to try even harder
Not to give in to the negatives.
Today may be a yawning trap of terribleness
But there's still tonight or tomorrow or ten years from
   now.

Sometimes, I'm afraid I could be
        Another Anna.

So, until I'm sure I believe it,
I'll say it 20 or 20,000 times.

I don't have to be Someone
To be someone special.
I don't have to live the dream
To believe in the future of my dreams.

Lanny Laring

A suicide.
Different.

A quick look around the room.
No one knows quite what to do.

For once, even Old Mason is silent.
Alexis looks like she's going to pass out.
Lynn looks almost mad.

Everyone's avoiding eye contact.
Except Aaron, of course,
He can't wait to earn another A today.

A suicide.
What's my slant?

Life's all about seeing the slants, analyzing the angles.
And it's so easy to play the part of winner.
Like the time I "accidentally" ran into Damon.
      As planned, it bruised his knee pretty badly.
      Greg got into the game,
      And I got ten bucks richer.
Or like the time I found Lauren's missing bracelet,
      She kissed me and called me super.

How could she ever know how easily I had stolen it?

So what's the angle in this suicide?

Showtime.

Another victory waits.

Michelle Magden

Every time my father sees me frown,
He says,
"Are you upset?
        You know you can talk to me."

Every time my father hears me mad at my friends,
He says,
"Are you lonely?
        You know you can talk to me."

Every time my father thinks I'm sad,
He says,
"Are you depressed?
        You know you can talk to me."

Ever since my father got custody,
He's been reading books about parenting.
When he read that one in three teens thinks of suicide,
My father made me repeat,
"Suicide is a permanent solution to a temporary problem."

I've told him,
        "Dad,
                Sometimes, I get irritated or angry.
                Sometimes, I feel stupid or sad.
                Sometimes, I feel left out or lonely.

But I am not,
    have never been,
        will never be
                Suicidal!"

Still, I cannot convince my dad.

Once he hears about Anna,
He'll never let me out of his sight.
His anxiety will destroy
The little bit of social life I have.

"I don't know why Anna didn't know,
But, Dad, I do . . .
Really, I do understand

      That 'suicide is a permanent solution
      To a temporary problem.'"

Jeff Cook

So my dad is sitting in the stands
When I score another basket.
And he hears this father tell his son,
    "Do you know that guy?"
And the kid answers,
      "Sure, everyone knows Jeff.
      He's only about the most popular person in the
        whole school.
      He's in everything, does everything, is
        everything."
And the dad says,
      "Well, that could be you when you're a senior."
And the kid rolls his eyes and answers,
      "Get real, Dad!"

My father can't wait to come home and tell me all this.
His chest is puffed out with pride
As he says, "How about that!"

I figure it's probably not the best time to inform him
That I do know everyone
And no one . . .
And a lot of the time,
What I really feel

Is alone.

Ms. Standring,
Attendance Secretary

"It wasn't my fault."
They should inscribe those words above this office
    door.
Then all the kids that come through it could just point.

Today's troops,
Most of them tardy or in trouble,
Wait unwillingly to see
Whether they'll get off
With only a warning from me
Or hit the big time and
Earn a detention from the dean.

But this day,
They'll all have to wait a little longer.
For as I hear them
            Joking,
                    Flirting,
                            Complaining,
                                    Cajoling,
I cannot stop imagining the silent forever that
Anna Gonzales has chosen.

"It wasn't my fault."

I know I'll hear that a hundred times today,
And I'll explain that—"Yes, it is your fault"—
Just as many times.

Life can be messy.
No doubt, a lot of these kids are living proof.
But in spite of their anxieties and their angers,
At least —
      They
         Are trying to live.

Jermaine Clements

Bomp . . . bada . . . bomp.
Bomp . . . bomp . . . bada . . . bomp.
This song has the beat
That makes my whole body move.
But I've got to stay still.

✓ No Walkmen
✓ No CD players
✓ No headphones
Allowed in this school.
I should know.
I've had enough of them confiscated.

But this earphone redefines miniature.
And the CD's so small, it slips unseen inside a pocket.
If I just sit staring at my teachers,
They'll never know
That I've tuned out their teaching tortures
With music that makes school rock.

Bomp . . . bomp . . . bada . . . bomp.
No doubt about it.
Technology is improving my education.

Julio Contraros

So many times have our families come together.
But Anna never seemed sad.
So many times when *mi madre* was uncertain of this
    new country
Was Anna's mother there to help us.
To translate until English we learned.
To explain so many customs new and strange.

I will go to *la casa de Gonzales* after this day of school.
But I do not know words in any language to help.

My heart cries for Anna
And for
Her mother
The friend and protector to us all.

Too late it is to help Anna.
And Señora Gonzales
Who can protect her
In this terrible tragedy?

Hay también mucha tristeza.
It is too much sadness.

Leslie Leiberman

Forget about that Biology X and Y stuff
About what makes a boy or a girl.
It's really much simpler.
Guys all have the jerk gene.
It's like God says, "Oh, that one gets a jerk gene;
    so it's a boy."

Like Sean Saunders.
After I baked him two batches of double-fudge
    brownies.
After I offered to watch his dog when his family went
    away for the weekend.
After I did his algebra because he was too tired from
    basketball.

Finally, this morning, right before the bell, he wants to
    ask me something,
My heart pounds, and I think this is it.
He's finally going to ask me to Homecoming.

But then the bell rings. He gets nervous and says,
    "Maybe later."
I worry that later may never happen,
So I practically shout, "Now . . . I mean I can afford
    the tardy."

He says, "You sure?"
And I say, "I'm sure . . . just ask . . ."
So he says, "Okay, do you know Kendra well enough
    to find out
If she'll go to Homecoming with me?"

And so now I've got this tardy.
And now I've got no date for Homecoming.

Fact: Guys are filled with jerk genes.
Fact: Sean Saunders has more than his share.

Sean Saunders

In Advanced Art, I made an A+ clay mask.
Perfect in its features, it revealed
    Interestingly shaped empty eyes
    A flawlessly impossible porcelain complexion
    And a mouth that exposed neither a smile
        nor a frown.

Holding my creation in front of me,
I look out from behind its cold indifference
Feeling no more anonymous than
The usual face I wear.

Each day, I carefully apply another
Mask to hide the mask
That almost worked
The day before.

Masked behind masks that mask
Anything that is real.
This is the only way a teenager
Survives the hell called
High school.

Anna, did your disguise slip
Or was it just that your eyes could
No longer find insight
Buried
Behind so many masks?

Kinderlyn Itovoticich

Anna . . .

I remember . . .

My first day of school in America.
Labeled a resettled refugee,
Lost in this upside-down place,
Students swirling by—talking a language
    that made no sense.
Me—huddling in a hallway
Feeling almost as anxious
As when I heard the sounds
Of bombs in my other world.

No one seemed to notice
But you, Anna.
Using signs and smiles,
You made sure I got to my classes.
Showed me how lunch worked,
How to open a jammed locker.
You taught me how to smile and
How to survive in junior high.

You were my first American friend.

I didn't mean to ignore you when we got to high school.
I really liked the badminton team I joined.
And it seemed so easy to sit at their lunch table,
Get in on their gossip, and be part of their parties.

So I told myself you had a lot of other friends.
I was the one who had been different.
And now it was probably a relief that
The "foreign kid" didn't need babysitting anymore.

But if I look deep enough inside myself,
I wonder if I'll find out that was a lie.
And I have no answer for
How could I have forgotten how
You once solved my fears
Before you even knew my name.

Maybe my lack of loyalty doesn't matter at all.
Maybe it had nothing to do with what you did.

But maybe if . . .

Oh, Anna . . .

Jordan Smythe

Once I had this jigsaw puzzle.
I worked on it every day.
It was the hardest thing I'd ever done,
But I finally got it all finished
Except for one piece,
Which was missing.
I looked for it everywhere,
Under my bed, behind the table, in the closet,
But the piece was just gone.
Pretty soon, when I looked at the puzzle
All I could see
Was the missing piece.
So I threw the whole thing away.
All my hard work, all my effort tossed in the
    garbage.
The next week I found the missing piece
But, of course, I no longer had the puzzle.

So why am I thinking about this puzzle today
When I hear about Anna Gonzales's suicide?

I don't know.

Maybe it's one of those metaphor things.

Andrew Stevenson,
Security Guard

"Security" it says in big yellow letters
That span the back of my blue staff shirt.
But I've always thought it should say "Insecurity"
Because that's what I create.

I want to make kids feel uneasy
About smoking,
Dealing drugs,
Cutting class, or
Sneaking out of school.
Yeah—I know I don't get them all,
But school statistics say I'm having an effect.

Most of the time, when I catch a kid, they just shrug,
Accepting that they played the game and lost.
But yesterday, at the southernmost exit of the school,
When I confronted a boy trying to skip out after
    second hour,
He started to shake.
Said he had a "personal problem."
Said it had to be handled now.
Begged me to just turn the other way
And let him leave.

I told him, "No can do—have your parents
    excuse you."
        "But I can't do that!" he shouted.

I told him, "Wait and handle it after school."
  "I can't do that either!" he choked.

He seemed really desperate,
But the rules are the rules.
So I told him, "Head back to class."
  "Please . . . ," he begged.
So I told him, "Go see your counselor."

His penetrating blue eyes
Stared at me in agony.
Then he turned and walked back into the school.

I did feel sorry for him,
Which was why
I didn't take his name.
I didn't haul him to the dean.
And I did tell him to go to his counselor.
That was the most I could do.

But the announcement about Anna Gonzales just
    ended,
And suddenly
That yesterday boy's face worries me,
As I wonder
Could I . . . should I . . .
Have done something more?

Andrew Stevenson, Security Guard   95

Jamie McSully

No

No

No

No

No

No

Oh God . . .

Anna Gonzales
(the Note)

I will slip away,
Making little fuss.
And being less remembered,
Which is pretty much the way I have always been.

Never pretty or popular enough to matter.
Never outrageous or outstanding enough
   to get attention.
Sometimes, I have to pinch myself to make certain
   that I am even real.
Conversations swirl around me.
Invitations to others surround me.
Even Alexis, who has tried to be my best friend,
Is dragged down by my invisibility.

No, I am not pregnant
Not on drugs
Not alcohol
Not influenced by rock or heavy metal or rap

I am just not.
And I am so tired of trying to be.

So I say my good-night to this world
Feeling since it has never embraced me
It will not mind if I have abandoned it.

About the author

Terri Fields was inspired to write this book by her feelings of despair over teenage suicide. She says, "Not only is it the end of a life and of hope for that life, but it also creates ongoing painful ripples in others' lives."

An award-winning author of sixteen books, Ms. Fields is an educator who has been named Arizona Teacher of the Year, and was selected for the All-USA Teacher Team of the nation's top educators. She lives with her family in Phoenix, Arizona.